THE AMAZING ADVENTURES OF

SCARY BONES
THE SKELETON

The Third Adventure

Scary Bones meets the
Dinosaurs of the Jurassic Coast

By

Ron Dawson

Illustrated by Sue Burleigh

i

D1584649

First Published in 2010 by Mulberry Tree Books

Copyright © Dr Ronald L Dawson 2010

Illustrations © Sue Burleigh 2010

Photographic images of Durdle Door with kind permission of Lulworth Castle and Estate. ©
Design, layout and colour work by Ron Dawson.

Dr R L Dawson has asserted his right under the Copyright Designs and Patents Act 1988 to be
identified as the author of this work.

All rights reserved. No part of this publication may be reproduced, stored in retrieval system, or
transmitted, in any form or by any means, electronic, mechanical, photocopying, recording, or
otherwise, without the prior permission of the author.

This novel is an original work of fiction, as are the characters portrayed in it. Any resemblance
to any persons living or dead is purely coincidental.

A CLP catalogue record of this book is available from the British Library.

Printed and bound in the UK by Imprintdigital, Exeter EX5 5HY.

'Hello! I'm a most unusual dinosaur because there has never been a dinosaur just like me since the whole wide world began. Find out who I am in this Scary Bones' adventure.'

MTBooks

Mulberry Tree Books, Mulberry House, Winterborne Stickland, Dorset DT11 0NT
www.mulberrytreebooks.co.uk

ISBN 978-0-9561732-4-9

The Third Adventure:
<u>Scary Bones</u> Meets the Dinosaurs of the Jurassic Coast

Chapter 1

Sasha and Ben were on holiday at the seaside and today their parents had taken them to the beach to search for fossils. After only a few moments of searching, Sasha called to her brother, Ben,

'Look Ben, I've found one,' and she held out what looked like a lump of rock for Ben to see.

Ben looked very closely at the lump of rock. 'Yes, I think it is,' he said. 'I think it really is a fossil. Well done Sasha!'

Sasha and Ben had learned that a fossil is all that is left of an animal which died millions and millions and millions of years ago, and perhaps even longer than that. After the animal died, it had been covered by layer after layer of mud and stone until its remains turned into solid rock.

'I wonder what it's the fossil of,' Ben said. 'It's all curly-wurly, just like a curly-wurly sea shell.'

'I've seen pictures of ones just like it in books,' Sasha answered. 'I think it's called an … am …mon…ite, yes that's it, it's an ammonite. They lived in the sea when the dinosaurs were alive. Millions and millions of them lived right here and so there are millions of their fossils on this beach.'

'And lots and lots of dinosaurs lived here too and there are lots of dinosaur fossils in those cliffs over there,' Ben said and pointed towards some grey cliffs which came right down to the beach where they were standing. 'That's why this is called the Jurassic coast, because Jurassic is what clever people who know everything about dinosaurs call the time when dinosaurs lived here, and that was millions and millions and millions of years ago, and perhaps even longer than that.'

'Come on Ben, let's go and see if we can find some fossils of dinosaurs on the cliffs,' Sasha said.

'Sasha, you know we were told not to climb on the cliffs because sometimes parts of them fall down and can be very dangerous,' Ben replied. But before the words had even left his mouth, Sasha had run over to the cliffs and was starting to scramble up them.

'Come on Ben,' she called to him. 'Don't be a scaredy scaredy custard, we might find a dinosaur fossil. And don't forget to bring Scary Bones' box!'

With a big sigh, *ppphhhhoooofff*, Ben picked up the grey box that Scary Bones the skeleton would sometimes pop out of and ran to the cliffs where Sasha was scrambling about high up on them.

Suddenly, as Ben looked up at Sasha, her feet slipped and she sent a shower of rocks crashing down the cliff towards where Ben was standing.

'Look out Ben,' Sasha shouted, 'look out!'

Ben saw the rocks tumbling and rumbling down the cliff towards him. Ben knew that if any of the rocks hit him he would be hurt very badly and so he jumped as far as he could to get out of their way. He was just in time and the rocks crashed on past him and down to the beach below without hitting him. But when Ben jumped to save himself, he dropped Scary Bones' box and it went tumbling down the cliffs after the falling rocks until it landed at the bottom of the cliff with a loud *rattle-ker-tum-dum-ker-rattle-ker-plonk*.

'Scary Bones, Scary Bones!' Sasha cried out. 'You've dropped the box with Scary Bones in it, Ben, he'll be smashed into millions and millions of little pieces.'

'I couldn't help it,' Ben answered with tears running down his face, 'I couldn't hold onto his box when I had to jump out of the way to escape from the falling rocks.'

Sasha and Ben scrambled down the cliff to where Scary Bones' grey box lay. As they got closer they saw the magical piece of Red String, which lived in the grey box, slither out and spread itself out on the rocks. It lay there shaking and quivering like someone who has been so frightened out of their wits that they can't get back into their wits because they are so frightened.

The children looked at the grey box in horror. Their parents had told them not to climb on the cliffs and because they had not done as they were told, they might have smashed their best friend into millions of pieces. The lid on the box shook and quivered and then, with a final shudder, fell off. They stared at the open box and crossed all of their fingers and toes and wished and wished and wished, and then wished once more for good luck.

As if in answer to their wishes, a golden glow began to appear in the box. It grew brighter and brighter until suddenly it went '*POP*' and there stood Scary Bones, Scary Bones the Skeleton, all in one piece, and he was as bright and as golden as he had ever been!

'Hoorah, hoorah, Scary Bones,' they shouted with delight. 'You are back and not hurt at all.'

'Well, perhaps a little bit shaken and stirred,' he said with one of his biggest toothiest smiles, 'but there are no bones broken, and let's face it, I have nothing else to break. What on earth happened?'

Sasha and Ben laughed with relief that Scary Bones was not hurt and because, as always, Scary Bones had said something that was so exactly true that it made them laugh.

'Oh, I'm so sorry Scary Bones,' said Ben, 'there were rocks falling towards me and I had to jump out of the way and when I did I dropped your box. I didn't mean to, really, it was an accident.'

'And I'm sorry too,' Sasha said. 'It was because I was climbing on the cliffs that the rocks tumbled down towards Ben,' and she pointed towards where the rocks had fallen from.

'Don't worry about it one little bone,' said Scary Bones. 'I was away in Skeleton Land when Ben dropped my box and so I haven't hurt even my littlest little bone.' Then Scary Bones turned to look at the rocks that Sasha was pointing towards. 'But what is that funny looking thing over there?' he asked and pointed his pointiest bony finger towards a large black curly something or other which was sticking out from the cliff.

'It's another ammonite,' Sasha said. 'It must have been uncovered by the rocks which have just fallen from the cliff. I found one just like it on the beach only a few minutes ago.'

'Yes, but it wasn't as big as that one,' Ben said, 'that one is as big as an extra big curly doorknob.'

'Let's take a closer look at it,' said Scary Bones, 'but be careful not to loosen any more rocks.'

So slowly and carefully the three of them climbed up to where the ammonite was sticking out from the cliff.

'See if you can pull it out, Ben,' Sasha said.

Ben grabbed the ammonite with both hands and pulled and pulled but it didn't move one little bit.

'Let me have a go,' said Scary Bones and he pulled and pulled on it too but it still didn't move even the littlest of little bits.

'Try to turn it, Scary Bones,' Sasha said, 'try to turn it like a doorknob,' and so Scary Bones gripped the ammonite as tightly as he could and tried to turn it like a doorknob.

Slowly but surely it began to turn and, as it did, they heard a mighty rumbling. It was as loud as the loudest thunder in the stormiest of storms on the darkest of dark nights and, all around them, the cliffs began to *crrraaaaaack, crrreeeeeeak* and *shuuuddderrrrrrrrrrrrrr.*

All around them, the whole cliff seemed to be making noises and moving and shaking. But it wasn't the whole cliff that was making noises and moving and shuddering. It was only the part right in front of them, and then they saw it. Right there, in front of their double-popping eyes, they saw a giant stone door appear out of the cliff and it was beginning to open.

Scary Bones was so surprised that he let go of the ammonite doorknob and he and the children stared at the door that was opening right in front of them. Even the Red String, which had got back into some of its wits and had recovered some of its puff, had slithered up behind them to take a look too.

The giant stone door opened wider and wider until it couldn't open any wider and came to a stop with a mighty clump. *K-kerrrllluuummmppp!*

The children could hardly believe their double-popping eyes and the Red String wrapped itself around one of Scary Bones' legs in surprise and fright. As the door clumped to a stop, all of the noises and rumblings and moving came to a stop too and the cliff became silent and still once more.

Scary Bones and the children crept towards the

giant doorway to see what was on the other side of it. When they looked through they could see a bright green valley with hills all around it. Some of the hills were little volcanoes which were puffing out puffs of white fluffy smoke. In the valley there were strange tall trees with long drooping branches and leaves. There were giant plants dripping with dew and there were steamy mists everywhere. The sky was a bright yellow and the sun was an even brighter green. It was the strangest and most beautiful valley the children had ever seen. It was nicer than the nicest dream that they had ever dreamed.

'We have found a lost world,' whispered Ben. 'And no-one knows that it's here but us.'

'Can we go in and explore it then?' said Sasha. 'Because if no-one know it's here, then nobody could have told us not to go in.'

'That is very true,' said Scary Bones, 'but even so I don't think we should go in there. Look what happened when you climbed up the cliff when you were told not to.'

But before Sasha could answer, the Red String had slithered through the giant door and was slithering away into the lost world. Without stopping to think, Sasha, Ben and Scary Bones went chasing after it to bring it back. But no sooner had they stepped through the giant door when they heard another mighty clump.

K-kkkerrrllluuummmppp!

The giant door had slammed shut behind them!

'Quickly, Ben,' Sasha shouted in fright. 'Find the ammonite doorknob and get us out of here!

Ben ran back to where the door had been but he couldn't see an ammonite doorknob anywhere. In fact he couldn't see anything that looked like a doorknob, or even a door, anywhere at all.

'Let me take a look,' said Scary Bones but he couldn't see anything like a door or a doorknob either. The door had become just one smooth slab of stone and they could not see how they would ever be able to find a way to get back through it.

'We're locked in,' Sasha cried. 'We are prisoners inside a lost world which no-one knows about, and if no-one knows about it, they will never be able to find us. We are locked in here forever!'

Ben and Scary Bones knew that Sasha was right. They were locked in a lost world and there was....

NO ESCAPE.

Chapter 2

The children and Scary Bones sat down on a rock and looked at the beautiful green valley below them. They were feeling very sad but right in front of them the Red String was hopping and dancing about. It was just like an excited puppy that is excited because it has been taken somewhere new and exciting. It was very clear that the Red String wanted to explore this new world and that it wanted them all to follow it.

'Perhaps it knows a way out of here,' said Sasha.

'How could it know a way out of here,' asked Ben, 'when it has never been in here before?'

'You never know where the Red String has been or where it hasn't been,' said Scary Bones, 'but we can't just sit here twiddling our thumbs.'

Sasha and Ben nodded their heads to agree and the three of them set off to follow the Red String as it slithered along a small pathway between the strange trees and plants. All around them they could hear strange noises, noises they had never ever heard before.

'*Wheerr-tweet-tweet. Knuck, knuck. 'Zzzzzzing Zzzzzzeerring. Brrrrrrmm brrrrrrmm. Pip pippety pip. Oooosssshh ooosssh. Oooah, oooah.*'

And although they couldn't see them, they felt as if thousands of eyes were watching them as they followed the Red String as it slithered along as happily as could be down the small path.

Then, suddenly, they heard something very big crashing its way through the plants and trees right behind them. *Crash, crash, crash, crash.*

Then out onto the path stepped the biggest big animal they had ever ever seen or were ever likely to see ever again. It was twice as tall as the biggest big elephant and twice as long as the biggest big whale. It had a tail twice as long as the biggest big snake and had twice as many teeth as the biggest big crocodile, but it had very tiny eyes. The whatever-it-was looked down the path and saw Scary Bones and the children. Then, with a wag of its big tail which knocked down two trees, it came bounding down the path towards them. *Clumpetty, clumpetty, clumpetty clump.*

The children screamed with fright and Scary Bones turned to a bright yellow, which is what skeletons do when they are very very frightened.

It was getting closer and closer and so all three of them began to run as fast as their legs and bones could carry them down the small path with the giant whatever-it-was chasing after them.

The Red String, which was slithering in front of them as fast as it could slither, suddenly slithered to a slithery stop. The children and Scary Bones knew this meant that they should stop too, but when they tried to stop, they just skidded on right past where the Red String had stopped and fell into a great big hole!

They landed at the bottom of the hole with a *bump*, that was Ben, then another *bump*, that was Sasha, and then a *rattle*, that was Scary Bones. As soon as they recovered from their bumps and rattles they stood up and looked around.

'Where are we?' asked Ben.

'We are in a hole,' Scary Bones answered.

Sasha and Ben couldn't help laughing. 'Yes, we know we are in a hole, but where is the hole?'

'It's in the ground,' Scary Bones answered.

'Yes, we know that too, but where is the ground that the hole is in?'

'Now you've got me into a right muddle,' Scary Bones replied, 'but do you know something?'

The children were puzzled and said, 'No, what?'

Scary Bones looked at them as if he had just won a super prize for super cleverness. 'Well, if I knew where we were then I would tell you right away.'

Although they were very frightened Sasha and Ben couldn't help laughing again.

'Well, let's take a look at this hole that we are in,' said Ben and they all looked around the big hole. It was the biggest big hole they had ever seen, let alone had ever fallen into, and worst of all, it was so deep that they could not see how they would ever be able to get out of it. They were in a big deep dark hole and there was... NO ESCAPE!

From up above them they could hear the big whatever-it-was getting closer and closer to the big hole. *Clumpetty, clumpetty, clumpetty clump.*

They jumped up and ran to the other end of the hole because they knew that if the big whatever-it-was couldn't stop either, it would fall into the hole and fall right on top of them. And they also knew that if it did fall on top of them, it would be so super heavy that it would flatten them flatter than three flat pancakes that have been flattened flat.

Clumpetty, clumpetty, clumpetty clump.

They held their breath and then they heard a long *sccrrreeeeeccccchhhhh*! The whatever-it-was didn't fall in and so it must have screeched to a stop just in time! So they all let go of their breath, *phheeewwwww*, and said, 'That was close!'

They looked up to the top of the hole to see what the whatever-it-was was going to do now. But it wasn't the whatever-it-was that they saw, it was two cavemen who were looking down at them.

At first Sasha and Ben thought they could recognise the two cavemen, but they weren't quite sure. One was long and thin with pointy ears. He was wearing a tall round black woolly hat which looked as if it had been made out of a camel's long nose. He had a long black fur cloak which dangled so far down his back that it nearly reached the floor. He looked a like a silly penguin.

The other caveman was short and round. He was wearing a yellow and black striped tiger skin and he had a yellow and black striped tiger tail around his head. He looked like a big plump silly wasp.

'Oh, oh, oh,' the tall thin one shouted with delight, 'what do you think we have caught in our dinosaur trap, Mr. Zaggy?'

The short plump one looked at Sasha, Ben and Scary Bones in turn and answered, 'I think we have caught some yummy yummy yummies for our tummy tummy tummies, Mr. Ziggy.' And the two cavemen began to laugh and dance about.

'There's nothing to laugh or dance about,' Sasha called out angrily to them. 'We want you to get us out of here!'

'Oh yes,' said the one called Zaggy, 'we'll get you out of there alright and when we do we're going to eat you all for our supper.'

'I want that one,' the one called Ziggy said and pointed at Ben.

'But I want that one,' said Zaggy. 'You can have that one,' and he pointed at Sasha.

'You always want the one I want,' said Ziggy.

'Well you always want the one I want,' said Zaggy.

'But you always get the one I want,' said Ziggy

'No I don't,' said Zaggy. 'It's you that always gets the one you want, well this time I want the one that I want.' Then he pointed at Scary Bones, 'Durdle Doorus can have that bony one.'

As Zaggy pointed at Scary Bones, the big whatever-it-was came and looked into the hole too. It had a big flat snout like a pig's and a very wide mouth so that, when it smiled, its smile stretched right around its snout and right back to two little holes where its ears should have been at the back of its head. It didn't look at all frightening now. It looked just like a great big happy hippopotamus!

'What in the whole lost world is that?' Ben called up to the cavemen and pointed to the whatever-it-was. 'What ever is it?'

Ziggy and Zaggy stopped arguing with each other and looked very snootily down at the children and Scary Bones.

'It is not an 'it',' Zaggy replied. 'It is a she, a girl and she is called Durdle Doorus. She is our very own pet dinosaur.' And Durdle Doorus nodded her head happily at Scary Bones and the children.

'She can't be a dinosaur,' Sasha called back. 'There haven't been any dinosaurs on the earth for millions and millions and millions of years, and perhaps even longer than that.'

'Well I don't know about that,' Ziggy called back, 'but I do know that there are lots and lots of dinosaurs around here. That's why we made this big hole that you have fallen into. It's one of our dinosaur traps. The dinosaurs will fall into it just like you have, and then we will eat them, just like we are going to eat you!' And the two cavemen began laughing and dancing together again.

The children and Scary Bones held each other in fright. The children were going to become a caveman's dinner and Scary Bones a dinosaur's dinner and there was ...... NO ESCAPE!

Then they saw that the smile on the face of Durdle Doorus was getting wider and wider, in fact she was beginning to giggle and giggle. Then they saw why. The Red String, which had not fallen into the hole, was tickling the toes on one of her feet! Her giggling became giggillier and giggillier and her long tail wagged wider and wider until .... *tthhhhwwwwaaaaaccckkkk*. Her great big tail bumped into Ziggy and Zaggy and knocked them both headfirst down into the hole.

They landed right at the bottom, first with a *bimp*, that was Ziggy, and then a *bump*, that was Zaggy.

Ziggy and Zaggy picked themselves up and they shouted angrily at Durdle Doorus. 'You clumsy big silly thing Durdle Doorus! Well now that you have knocked us down here, you can jolly well get us out!'

The Red String stopped tickling Durdle Doorus and she stopped giggling. She looked down at Ziggy and Zaggy and she wasn't even smiling anymore. Instead she looked very sad. She hadn't knocked them into the hole on purpose so why were they so angry with her? She turned around and she plodded off very sadly down the little path. *Ploddy, ploddy, ploddy…..*

'Now look what you've done,' said Zaggy, 'You have upset her and she has plodded off in a huff!'

'It wasn't me that upset her,' Ziggy replied, 'it was you!'

'Well it wasn't me that sent her off in a huff,' said Zaggy, 'it was you!'

'I didn't send her off in a huff,' said Ziggy, 'you did!'

'Oh no I didn't,' said Zaggy, 'it was you!'

'Oh no it wasn't,' said Ziggy, 'it was you!'

Scary Bones realised that Ziggy and Zaggy might argue like this with each other for ever and ever, and perhaps even longer than that, and so he shouted at them, 'Stop, stop! Never mind who upset Durdle Doris, or whatever her silly name is, or who sent her off in a huff, the point is that we are all in the same big hole now, and we all need to get out of it.'

Ziggy and Zaggy were so surprised when Scary Bones shouted at them that they stopped arguing with each other and looked around the big hole.

'It is a very big hole,' said Ziggy.

'A very very big hole,' said Zaggy. 'We made it so big so that only the biggest of big dinosaurs could ever escape from it.'

'So you see,' said Ziggy to the children and Scary Bones, 'if only the biggest of big dinosaurs could ever escape from it, then we will never to be able to escape from it. I'm very sorry to have to tell you that we are trapped in this hole for ever and ever and perhaps even longer than that. I'm very sorry to say that for us there is …….. NO ESCAPE!'

Chapter 3

Trapped at the bottom of the great big hole, they all sat down together and were very sad.

'I told you that we shouldn't have made the hole so big,' Ziggy said quietly to Zaggy.

'Oh no you didn't,' said Zaggy. 'It was me who said stop digging but you wouldn't stop.'

'Oh you fibbing fibber!' said Ziggy. 'I said stop but you said dig it bigger and bigger.'

'Oh you fibbing fibber yourself!' said Zaggy. 'It was you that wanted to dig it bigger and bigger.'

'Fibbing fibber!' said Ziggy. 'It was you.'

'Oh no it wasn't, you fibbing fibber!' said Zaggy. 'It was you.'

'Oh no it wasn't, it's you that is the fibbing fibber!' said Zaggy.

'Don't you dare call me a fibbing fibber you fibbing fibber!' said Ziggy.

'Stop, stop!' Scary Bones cried. 'Stop arguing and be quiet. I think I can hear something coming.'

Ziggy and Zaggy stopped arguing with each other and they all listened very carefully. *Clump, tipsy, clump, tipsy, clump, tipsy* ……..

'It's Durdle Doorus,' Zaggy cried with delight. 'She's coming back and it sounds as if she is bringing someone with her!'

They all looked up and saw Durdle Doorus looking down at them and smiling one of her biggest big smiles. Then a tiny head with big eyes and an even bigger smile followed by the longest long neck ever seen in the whole wide lost world came poking out over the hole right above them.

'What in the lost world is it?' Sasha asked Ziggy and Zaggy.

'It is not an 'it',' Ziggy replied very snootily. 'She is a girl too, and she is called Dippy Ludicrous. She is a cousin of Durdle Doorus and she is a dinosaur as well.'

The two dinosaurs sat looking into the hole wagging their big long tails like two happy giant puppies. Ziggy and Zaggy, however, were not quite so happy. Ziggy called up to them.

'Don't just sit there wagging your silly tails and looking at us, do something to get us out of here!'

'They're not silly tails,' said Zaggy. 'They are big and long but they are not silly.'

'Well I think that they are so big and so long that it makes them silly,' said Zaggy.

'Well if they are silly, then so are you!' said Ziggy.

'Then you are silly too!' said Zaggy.

'Don't you dare say that I am silly,' said Ziggy.

'Well I do dare and you are silly,' said Zaggy.

'Well if I am silly, I'm not as silly as you are,' said Ziggy.

'Oh yes you are, you are much sillier than me,' said Zaggy.

'Oh no I'm not ……..'

'Stop, stop,' Scary Bones shouted at them again. 'Calling each other silly names won't get us out of this silly hole. Now look at what the Red String is doing, I think it must have a cunning plan.'

Ziggy and Zaggy and the children looked up. The Red String was swaying backwards and forwards and from side to side like a snake on the tip of Dippy's nose and right in front of her big eyes.

'The Red String is trying to send Dippy to sleep,' Scary Bones said quietly and he began to sing softly and lightly in time with the Red String's dancing.

'Go to sshleeeeep, go to sshleeeeeep,
Dippy close your eyes, and
Go to ssssshhlleeeeeeepppp.'

Soon Dippy's big eyes began to sway in time with Scary Bones' singing and the Red String's dance, and then they began to close. She was falling asleep. As she fell asleep her long long neck with her head right at the end of it began to droop. Down and down it drooped taking her head with it until it and her tiny head came to rest right at the bottom of the hole where Scary Bones, the children and Ziggy and Zaggy were standing.

'Right,' Scary Bones called out. 'Quickly now. Everyone climb up Dippy's neck and escape from the hole. Come on, Sasha and Ben first.'

Sasha and Ben scrambled up Dippy's long neck until they were able to jump off at the top of the hole.

'Right,' said Scary Bones, 'now you Ziggy, up you go.'

'But I want to go next,' said Zaggy.

'Well you can't go next,' said Ziggy, 'because I'm going next.'

'You are always going first, said Zaggy, 'I never go first.'

'Yes you do,' said Ziggy. 'Only yesterday you went first.'

'Yes, but I only went first because you didn't want to go first,' said Zaggy.

'I did want to go first, but you went first instead,' said Ziggy. 'You always go first.'

' No I don't,' sad Zaggy. 'You always ……….'

'Stop, stop,' Scary Bones cried. 'If Dippy wakes up then no one will go first. So both of you, go now and go quickly!'

Ziggy and Zaggy climbed up Dippy's long neck arguing and pushing and pulling at each other until they were able to jump off at the top of the hole. Scary Bones was the last to climb out and as he did Dippy woke up.

When they were all safely out of the hole they all gave three big cheers for the Red String. 'Hoorah, hoorah, hoorah!'

'Right,' said Ben. 'We're out of the hole but which way do we go now?'

'Oh, we know which way to go, don't we Zaggy?' Ziggy said and gave Zaggy a big wink.

'Oh yes,' said Zaggy and big winked back at Ziggy. 'We'll show you which way to go. Just follow us.' And with that he and Ziggy began dancing in a ziggy-zaggy way down a little path.

'Why do you keep crossing from side to side?' asked Sasha. 'Why don't you dance in a straight line?'

'It's for our safety,' answered Zaggy. 'You see, there are two dinosaur brothers, Tyrone O'Saurus and Albert O'Saurus, and they are the biggest and fiercest of the biggest and fiercest dinosaurs. They are also very very heavy, in fact they are so heavy that, when they run very quickly, they can't stop or turn this way or that way very quickly at all.'

'So you see,' said Ziggy, 'when they chase us, if we make a surprise quick turn, they just run straight on and straight past us. So that's why we always ziggy-zaggy when we walk, run or dance, and that's why we are called Ziggy and Zaggy, because we're always ziggy-zaggying.'

'And now our good friends,' said Zaggy winking at Ziggy, 'we have a surprise turn for you!' And with that Ziggy untied a rope that was tied to a long bendy branch of a tree. As the rope untied, there was a loud '*Whhhooooooosssssshhhhhh*!'

Before they had time to think or blink, and perhaps in less time than that, Sasha, Ben and Scary Bones were *whooooshed* up high into the tree tops. They found that they were trapped inside a big net that had been fixed to the long bendy branch Ziggy had untied the rope from. They knew right away that they had been caught in another of Ziggy and Zaggy's dinosaur traps.

They pulled and tugged at the net but it was no
use. They were dangling in a big net so high up
among the tree tops that they knew that this time
there really was .... **NO ESCAPE!**

HERE'S ZIGGY and ZAGGY

Here's Ziggy and Zaggy, they are two, not a pair,
If Ziggy says, 'Here', Zaggy says, 'There'.
If Zaggy says, 'Yes', Ziggy says, 'No,'
And when Ziggy says, 'Stop,' Zaggy says, 'Go.'

When Zaggy says, 'Black,' Ziggy says, 'White,'
When Ziggy says, 'Left,' Zaggy says, 'Right.'
If Zaggy says, 'Day,', Ziggy says, 'Night,'
If Ziggy says, 'Dark,' Zaggy says, 'Light.'

When Zaggy says, 'Short,' Ziggy says, 'Long,'
When Ziggy says, 'Right,' Zaggy says, 'Wrong.'
But if Zaggy says, 'Me!' then Ziggy says, 'Me!'
And that's the only time that they ever agree!

Chapter 4

Trapped high among the tree tops in the net, the children and Scary Bones looked down at Ziggy and Zaggy. The two cavemen were dancing and singing again and this is what they were singing :

I am Ziggy, fol-de-roll,
I am Zaggy, fol-de-roll,
We're Ziggy and Zaggy, fol-de- roll,
And we'll eat you for supper!

And they laughed. 'Ha ha, ha ha, haaaaaaaaaa,' and began to sing the song again.

But then, slowly but surely, Ziggy and Zaggy stopped dancing, singing and laughing and looked up at the children and Scary Bones dangling inside the net high up among the tree tops. They had worried looks on their faces.

'Right Ziggy,' said Zaggy. 'Get the net down so that we can eat them for our supper.'

'No, you get it down,' said Ziggy. 'It's your turn.'

'No it's not my turn,' said Zaggy. 'It's your turn.'

'Oh no it's not, it's your turn,' Ziggy replied and then, looking straight at Zaggy, said, 'you don't know how to get the net down do you?'

'Yes I do,' said Ziggy. 'I just wanted to see if you knew how to do it.'

'Well I do know how,' said Zaggy, 'so you do it.'

'Oh no, I'm not going to,' said Ziggy, 'you do it.'

'Stop, stop,' Scary Bones called down to them. 'Neither of you know how to get us down, do you? You've caught us in another of your silly traps and now you can't get us out of it, can you?'

Ziggy and Zaggy nodded their heads and sat down on a rock looking very, very ashamed of themselves.

'I told you we shouldn't have made it so high,' said Zaggy.

'Oh no you didn't, you fibbing fibber!' said Ziggy, 'I wanted to ....'

'Stop, stop,' Scary Bones called to them again. 'Instead of arguing with each other, try to think of a way to get us down safely and to get us out of here!'

'Well come on then,' Zaggy said to Ziggy. 'Think of a way to get them down.'

'Why should I have to think of a way to get them down?' said Ziggy. 'Why don't you think of a way? It's always me ......'

Ziggy didn't finish what he was going to say because at that moment there was a great clumping and crashing and smashing and roaring and all sorts of frightening noises coming towards them from out of the trees. Then Durdle Doorus and Dippy Ludicrous came running out from the trees just in front of where the loudest noises were coming from. And then, running right behind them, came what was making the frightening noises....... two giant monster dinosaurs.

They were as tall as the tallest tall tree that ever grew and they walked on the longest long legs that ever walked. They had great big mouths filled with rows and rows of sharp teeth and, instead of hands, they had big claws like sharp hooks.

Ziggy and Zaggy stopped arguing at once and jumped to their feet.

'Oh, no!' they screamed in fright. 'It's the terrible O'Saurus brothers, Tyrone O'Saurus and Albert O'Saurus. If they catch us they will eat us all for their supper.' And with that, Ziggy and Zaggy ran away, ziggy-zaggying as fast as they could through the trees after Durdle and Dippy. They left Scary Bones and the children dangling in the net right in front of Tyrone and Albert's eyes as if they had been left as a monster dinosaur's tasty snack.

'Come back,' Scary Bones and the children shouted after Ziggy and Zaggy. 'Please come back and save us from becoming a dinosaur's supper!'

'We can't save you,' Ziggy and Zaggy called back to them. 'It's too late, it's too late. There's NO ESCAPE!'

When Tyrone and Albert saw the children and Scary Bones inside the net they stopped chasing after Ziggy and Zaggy and Durdle Doorus and Dippy. Instead they began to walk round and round Scary Bones and the children hanging helplessly in the net.

Their wicked eyes glinted, they smacked their giant red lips and they licked their rows and rows of sharp white teeth. Round and round they went, trying to decide which of the children or Scary Bones would be their first supper. For Scary Bones and the children there was ...NO ESCAPE!

When Ziggy and Zaggy realised that Tyrone and Albert had stopped chasing them, they stopped ziggy-zaggying and looked back. They saw that Tyrone and Albert were getting their big mouths and their rows and rows of sharp white teeth ready to take their first bite into the net.

'We are very sorry,' Ziggy and Zaggy called to them. 'We can't do anything to save you, but we know someone who might be able to save you.'

'Who is it?' the children called out. 'Tell us quickly who it is so that we can call for them to come and save us.'

'His name is Terry,' Ziggy and Zaggy called back. 'Terry Dactil, and he doesn't like Tyrone or Albert one little bit. Call for Terry, he might be able to save you because he can fly!'

'What do you think Scary Bones?' the children asked.

'Well we've got nothing to lose,' Scary Bones replied. 'It's worth a try.' And with that he began to shout as loudly as any skeleton has ever shouted since the first skeleton ever shouted loudly. 'Terry, Terry Dactil, please save us from Tyrone and Albert.'

But as you know, skeletons don't have any breathing bits inside them, and so although Scary Bones' shouting was very loud for a skeleton, he would never be able to shout as loudly as two noisy children who can shout loudly, or even one noisy child who can shout loudly for that matter.

And so Sasha and Ben began to shout too.

'TEERRRYY, TEERRRYY DAAAACCTILLLL, PLEASE SAVE US FROM THE MONSTERS TYRONE AND AL---BEEERRRTT!'

The suddenness and great loudness of their shouting surprised Tyrone and Albert so much that they jumped backwards and only their long tails stopped them from tumbling right over. When they realised that the loud noise was only coming from two children shouting, they came back to the net and got ready to eat their suppers.

They were just about to take their first big bite at the net when, from high in the sky, came a strange sound.

'Aaaaaaarrrrrrrrrllllllllleeeeeeeennnnnnneeeennnnn wwwwhhhhhooooooosssssshhh.'

It sounded like a fast flying aeroplane but the children knew that it could not be an aeroplane. When they looked up to see where the sound was coming from, they saw that it was coming from a giant flying something-or-other which was diving out of the sky straight towards them.

They knew that it couldn't be a dinosaur because they knew that dinosaurs can't fly. They knew that it couldn't be a bird because, although it could fly and had long wings, it didn't have any feathers. It had a long sharp beak that glinted like a knife in the sunlight, and little dangly legs with claws like hooks. Although they didn't know just what it was, the children guessed that, whatever the something-or-other was, it must be Terry Dactil and that he was coming to save them! 'Hoorah, hoorah,' they shouted. 'Terry Dactil is coming to save us!'

Tyrone and Albert saw him coming too and ducked their heads just in time for him to miss them. Terry skimmed by their heads and went flying straight past towards the net. He was flying far too fast to be able to stop but he was able to turn upwards towards the sky again. As he flew up past the net, his long sharp beak sliced right through the rope that was holding the net high up in the trees.

The net, with the children and Scary Bones in it, would have crashed to the ground but the Red String, which had been trying to untie the net from the tree, quickly hooked three of the net's ropes around Terry's beak. So, instead of crashing to the ground, the net was whisked away up into the sky hooked to the end of Terry's sharp beak.

Down on the ground Ziggy and Zaggy were cheering and shouting at the very top of their voices. 'Hoorah, hoorah, Terry Dactil has saved our suppers for us!'

Then they noticed, however, that although Terry had saved their suppers from Tyrone and Albert, he wasn't going to give them back to them. Instead he was flying away with their suppers inside the net which was dangling from the end of his beak!

'After him,' they shouted and they began chasing after Terry, the net and their suppers. Durdle and Dippy didn't want to be left out of the fun and so they began to chase after Ziggy and Zaggy. Tyrone and Albert were so angry about having a tasty supper stolen from right before their eyes that they began chasing after Durdle and Dippy, as they chased after Ziggy and Zaggy, as they chased after Terry and the net with the children and Scary Bones inside. It seemed as if everything in the lost world was chasing after everything else in the lost world.

Now although Scary Bones, the children and the Red String had escaped from Ziggy and Zaggy, and from Tyrone and Albert, they were still in great danger. They were still trapped inside the net but now it was flying even higher in the sky and dangling from only three ropes hooked around Terry's beak. The great danger was that Terry's beak was so sharp that it was cutting through the ropes one at a time!

'*Ddwwwrrraaaang-duummfff.*' Terry's beak cut through the first of the three ropes.

'*Ddwwwrrraaaang-duummfff.*' Terry's beak cut through the second of the three ropes.

The net was now only hooked to Terry's beak by one rope! When that was cut, the net, with them trapped inside it, would fall from the sky and go crashing to the ground below. There was nothing that they could do but watch in horror as Terry's sharp beak began cutting through the last rope.

'Quickly,' said Scary Bones. 'Let me lie at the bottom of the net and you climb on top of me.'

'But why?' asked Sasha and Ben.

'No time to tell you right now,' said Scary Bones, 'just do what I say quickly.'

Just as the children had done what Scary Bones had said there was another '*Ddwwwrrraaaang-dummfff.*' The third rope had been cut through! With no ropes to hold it, the net fell from Terry's beak and went crashing to the ground below.

'*Crrraaasshhh-rattle-rattle-bumpity-bump-rattle*'.

As it hit the ground the net burst open and Scary Bones, who had been lying at the bottom of the net, was smashed to pieces. All of his bones came apart and were thrown here, there and every-where. By lying at the bottom of the net with the children lying on top of him, Scary Bones had saved Sasha and Ben from being hurt at all but he himself had been completely bashed apart.

Sasha and Ben looked in horror at his bones which were scattered here, there and every-where all around them.

'Oh, poor Scary Bones,' they cried. 'You saved us but look what has happened to you. Now it's our turn to save you. We will put you back together again as quickly as we can, we promise.'

But at that very moment, two mighty roaring sounds echoed all around them.

'*Ggrrrrreeooooorrrrrrr, gwwwwrrrrriiiiaaaaannnn,*'

The roars were followed by two dark shadows. It was the two monster dinosaurs, Tyrone and Albert. They were back. They walked around and around Sasha and Ben smacking their big red lips and licking their rows and rows of big sharp white teeth. The children were frightened so much that they couldn't move. They were frozen to the spot.

Just as it seemed that there was no escape, a circle of rope dropped over Ben's shoulders and then another dropped over Sasha's. The ropes tightened and they were both yanked away from the monster dinosaurs just as they were about to be eaten. As they flew up into the air on the end of the ropes they heard two loud voices call out.

'These are our suppers Tyrone and Albert, you can eat those bones that are lying about here, there and everywhere or go and find something else to eat, but these two suppers belong to us!'

It was Ziggy and Zaggy and they were sitting on the back of Dippy Ludicrous as if they were riding a horse. They pulled the ropes up and up towards them until Sasha and Ben landed on Dippy's back right behind them.

'Right. Giddy yap Dippy, Giddy yap!' shouted Zaggy. 'Giddy yap as fast as you can giddy yap!'

Dippy rose up on her back legs and then set off at a full giddy yap with Ziggy, Zaggy and the two children hanging on as tightly as they could.

Tyrone and Albert were very very angry that their two tasty suppers were being snatched away from them and so they began to chase after Dippy determined to get their two suppers back.

As Dippy giddy yapped away, Sasha and Ben realised that without their help Scary Bones would never be able to put himself back together again and so they called out to him.

'Don't worry Scary Bones, we'll be back as soon as we can escape. We won't leave the lost world without you, we promise!'

But although they made that promise to Scary Bones, because they were tied up and captured by Ziggy and Zaggy and were being chased by Tyrone and Albert, the children really knew that there was little, if any, chance of them ever escaping or of saving Scary Bones.

Chapter 5

The sounds of Sasha and Ben's shouting and the noises of three dinosaurs crashing their way through the trees soon died away. Scary Bones' head looked around in silence. His bones were scattered here, there and everywhere. All of them had turned a sad grey because they knew, like him, that there was nothing Scary Bones could ever do to put himself back together again.

Then, in the silence, Scary Bones heard a huffing and a puffing noise and saw that it was coming from the Red String. The Red String was trying as hard as it could to pull and push his bones together again. But it was useless. The Red String just wasn't able to pull or push his bones anywhere, let alone click them together again. It seemed as if Scary Bones' only hope of ever getting back together again had gone.

The Red String slithered across to Scary Bones' head and snuggled up to it. There was nothing they could do but wait and hope for something to happen...... and then it did.

They heard the sounds of crying coming towards them. '*Boo hoo hooo, blubby blubby, sshhnniveell sshhnniveell,*' and out from the trees stepped Durdle Doorus. It was Durdle Doorus who they could hear crying and she was crying so much that her tears were running like rivers from her tiny eyes and falling like waterfalls from the edges of her big wide snout.

Now as you probably know, one of the cleverest things ever about skeletons is that they can speak to anything, anything at all, that has a skeleton inside them. And like all dinosaurs, Durdle Doorus had a skeleton inside her.

'What in the lost world is the matter, Durdle Doorus?' Scary Bones' head asked her.

'Who said that?' said Durdle Doorus nearly jumping out of her big skin with surprise because she couldn't see anyone or anything around her at all except a lot of grey bones lying here, there and everywhere.

'I did,' said Scary Bones' head. 'It was me, look, I'm down here.'

Durdle Doorus looked down and saw it was Scary Bones' head that was talking to her.

'Oh yes, there you are. I remember seeing you in Ziggy and Zaggy's big hole but you seem to have come apart at the joints since I last saw you.'

'Yes, I do seem to be in several places at once, but don't worry about me,' said Scary Bones, 'why are you crying so? Why are you so very unhappy?'

'It's that Ziggy and Zaggy!' she replied with a sniff and a snivel. 'They blame me for everything that goes wrong. They say that I'm clumsy and silly and they call me hurtful names. And now they have thrown me out. They say that they don't want to see me anymore. Dippy is their pet dinosaur now and they have said that she can't be my friend anymore, and so I'm all alone. I don't have any friends or anyone to care for me at all,' and she started to cry again, '*boo hoo hoooooooo.*'

'Oh, please don't cry Durdle,' said Scary Bones. 'You're not all alone because I'm here and I'll be your friend.'

Durdle stopped crying at once and a great big smile spread across her big face right round from her big snout to her tiny ears so that she looked just like a great big happy hippopotamus again.

'Will you really?' she said. 'Cross your heart and everything?'

'If I had anything to cross at all I would cross it right away,' Scary Bones' head replied, 'because I like you and I really would like to be your friend, I promise. You will just have to trust me'.

'Oh, I'm so happy to have a real friend at last,' said Durdle and she wagged her big long tail with delight. 'Now really good friends should always try to help each other, so is there anything I can do to help you?'

'Well I would like to be put back together again,' Scary Bones replied, 'but I think that you might be far too big to be able to do that for me.'

Durdle smiled and wagged one of her big front legs towards Scary Bones' head. 'I think that you think that I am be too big and clumsy to do it, don't you?' she said. 'But I'm not clumsy at all when I choose not to be you know. I'll show you. Now tell me which of your bones fit to which and I'll put you back together again in no time at all.'

'Well I have a little song which might help you to put me back together again,' he said and he began to sing his '*Put Scary Bones Back Together Song*' and, because Durdle Doorus was so very big, he sang it very very slowly.

The Put Scary Bones Back Together Song

'Oh my toe bones are connected to my...
   foot bones,
My foot bones are connected to my...
   ankle bones,
My ankle bones are connected to my...
   shin bones,
My shin bones are connected to my...
   knee bones,
My knee bones are connected to my...
   thigh bones,
My thigh bones are connected to my...
   hip bones,
My hip bones are connected to my...
   back bones,
My back bones are connected to my...
   shoulder bones,
My shoulder bones are connected to my...
   arm bones,
My arm bones are connected to my...
   wrist bones,
My wrist bones are connected to my...
   hand bones,
Now Scary can use his hands to
   connect his neck to his... back bones
And now he can connect his head to his...
   neck bones,
And Scary Bones is back together again!
        Hoorah!'

As Scary Bones began to sing, Durdle lifted herself up onto the tippiest tips of her great big toes as if she were a beautiful ballerina. Then, moving in time with the music, she used her long tail, just like an elephant uses its trunk, to pick up the bones and click them together. She carried on picking and clicking until she had picked and clicked every one of Scary Bones' bones back together. And when she had finished and Scary Bones was all back together again, he turned to a bright golden colour which showed that he was very very happy.

'There, I told you I could do it,' Durdle said proudly and she smiled her biggest big smile ever.

'And so you did,' cried Scary Bones and threw his arms as far as he could around Durdle's big neck and gave her the toothiest kiss anyone could ever be given by a skeleton. The Red String was so happy that it jumped from Scary Bones' head onto Durdle's head and danced about on it to show that it was Durdle's friend too.

'Oh, I'm so happy. We are real friends now and all of your friends are now my friends too,' cried Durdle, 'and so now I must help you to rescue those two children who are friends of yours. Come on, I'll take you to where I know Ziggy and Zaggy will have taken them.'

With that, Durdle Doorus gently picked up Scary Bones with her long tail and put him on her back as if he were riding an elephant. The Red String slithered down from Durdle's head and curled itself around the top of Scary Bones' head.

'Hold on tight, because here we go!' Durdle said and off she trotted into the trees to rescue Sasha and Ben, although she didn't know quite exactly how, or even if, she and Scary Bones would be able to rescue them.

With Scary Bones and the Red String riding on her back, Durdle Doorus trotted off as quickly and as quietly as she could down a pathway between the tall trees. She knew that Ziggy and Zaggy would have taken Sasha and Ben to their hidden cave and she knew exactly where that was.

She also knew that Tyrone and Albert would be looking for Ziggy and Zaggy because Ziggy and Zaggy had snatched Sasha and Ben away from them just as they were about to eat them for their supper.

After a while Scary Bones leant forwards and whispered into one of Durdle's tiny ears, 'Just stand still for a moment, Durdle, and be very quiet. I think I can hear something.'

Durdle Doorus stopped and they all listened very carefully.

'Keep very still now, Durdle,' Scary Bones whispered to her, 'I'll see if I can see anything.'

Scary Bones rose to his feet very slowly and very quietly until he was standing on tip-toe on the very top of Durdle's head. 'That's good,' he whispered. 'I can see over the trees now.'

'What can you see?' whispered Durdle.

'I can see Ziggy and Zaggy in front of a cave at the top of a hill,' he answered. 'And they have put Sasha and Ben into a big pot full of water and they are putting wood and sticks all around it.' Then Scary Bones realised what Ziggy and Zaggy were going to do. 'They are making a fire under the pot to boil Sasha and Ben alive and then they are going to eat them for their supper! Listen to what they are singing.'

Durdle Doorus and Scary Bones listened in horror as Ziggy and Zaggy sang and danced around Sasha and Ben inside the big pot of water.

This is what they were singing :

> '*I am Ziggy, fol-de-roll,*
> *I am Zaggy, fol-de-roll,*
> *We're Ziggy and Zaggy, fol-de- roll,*
> *And we'll boil you for supper.*'

For Sasha and Ben there was **NO ESCAPE!**

'Right,' said Ziggy, 'it's time for me to light the fire.'

'But you lit the fire last time,' said Zaggy. 'It's my turn to light this fire.'

'Oh you flipping fibbing fibber, you lit the last fire,' said Ziggy. 'Now it's my turn to light the fire, I want to light this fire.'

'I didn't light the last fire,' said Zaggy, 'you did! So if anyone is a flipping fibbing fibber, it's you, not me. It's my turn to light the fire. I want to light it.'

'I'm not a flipping fibbing fibber, you are a flipping fibbing fibber, you are always telling big flipping fibbing fibs,' said Zaggy

'No I'm not, you are.' said Ziggy. 'You told even bigger flipping fibbing fibs when.......'

Ziggy and Zaggy were arguing so much that they didn't notice that Tyrone and Albert, who were hiding in the trees, had crept up right behind them. Dippy, who was supposed to be keeping a look out, hadn't noticed them either.

Suddenly, Tyrone and Albert jumped out from the trees and roared, "*Ggrreeoorr, Gwwrriiaannn.'*

Ziggy and Zaggy were so surprised that they stopped arguing with each other at once.

'Oh no! It's Tyrone and Albert,' Ziggy cried in fright. 'Run for it, Zaggy, run for it!'

'But what about our suppers?' asked Zaggy.

'They will have to look after themselves,' Ziggy shouted. 'We've got to save ourselves. Run, run!'

'But what about Dippy?' called Zaggy. 'Tyrone and Albert might eat her too!'

'Well she will have to look after herself too!' Ziggy replied, 'We've got ourselves to look after. Run, for it, run!'

And Ziggy and Zaggy ran off ziggy-zaggying down a steep pathway on the other side of the hill leaving Sasha and Ben to be eaten by Tyrone and Albert.

The two monster dinosaurs stomped across to the big pot to see what Ziggy and Zaggy were cooking for their supper. Stomp, stomp, stomp. Sasha and Ben heard the monsters stomping towards them and so, after taking two deep breaths, ducked their heads under the water.

When Tyrone and Albert looked into the pot all that they could see was water with nothing in it at all for them to eat. Then they looked at Dippy and wondered if they could eat Dippy for their supper. Dippy, however, was very very big and so, like all big bullies, they thought that she might be a little too big for them to fight. It seemed their only chance of catching a supper without a big fight was to catch Ziggy and Zaggy. They could see Ziggy and Zaggy ziggy-zaggying down the steep hill and so they set off to chase after them.

Scary Bones had been watching all of this by standing on the top of Durdle's head. As soon as the monsters ran off to chase after Ziggy and Zaggy, he jumped down onto Durdle's back and shouted, 'Giddyap Durdle, there's no-one but Dippy at the cave now and so we can rescue Sasha and Ben!'

Durdle set off as quickly as she could and they soon reached the cave. Scary Bones jumped from her back and ran to the big pot. He tapped on the side of it, '*Tap, tap,*' and he called out quietly, 'Sasha. Ben. It's me, Scary Bones.'

Two heads popped up from the water in the pot. They were Sasha and Ben's and they were spluttering and squirting water from out their mouths, noses and ears. They wouldn't have been able to hold their breath under the water for a moment longer.

'Quickly,' Scary Bones called to them. 'Get out of the pot as quickly as you can! We need to escape before Tyrone and Albert come back!'

Sasha and Ben tried to climb out of the pot but the sides were too steep and too wet and too slippery for them to climb out. No matter how they tried they just couldn't get out of the big pot. There was .... NO ESCAPE!

Dippy Ludicrous had been watching all of these goings on without doing or saying anything. She was feeling very sad for herself. Ziggy and Zaggy had told her that they were her friends but they had run away and left her to face the terrible Tyrone and Albert on her own. She also realised now how her old friend Durdle Doorus must have felt when Ziggy and Zaggy threw her out and she felt very ashamed of herself that she had not stayed a friend to Durdle. But now she had a chance of showing Durdle and all the others that she was not like Ziggy and Zaggy. She was the sort of dinosaur who would help her friends when they were in trouble and needed help.

She thought for a moment and then lowered her long neck down into the pot for Sasha and Ben to hold on to. It was just like when she had rescued them from the big hole. When they were holding on to her neck, she lifted them out of the pot and lowered them safely down to the ground.

'Three cheers for Dippy,' cried Scary Bones and they all cheered as loudly as they could, 'Hip hip, hoorah, hoorah, hoorah!'

But they cheered too soon because, at the bottom of the steep hill, Tyrone and Albert heard their loud cheering and turned around to see where it was coming from. When they saw it was coming from Sasha, Ben and Scary Bones, they began to run back up the steep hill as fast as they could. They were so big and could run so fast that Scary Bones and the children knew that neither they, nor Durdle, nor Dippy, could ever run as fast as the monsters. There was .... NO ESCAPE!

Albert O'Saurus

Chapter 6

Tyrone and Albert were getting nearer and nearer to the top of the hill. Scary Bones and the children shivered and shook with fright. Tyrone and Albert could run so fast, even up hill, that running away would be useless and they couldn't think of anything else to do. There was NO ESCAPE. They were all going to become a dinosaur's supper.

But then, without making a sound, Durdle Doorus trotted towards the big pot of water. As she got nearer to it she began to run faster and faster. Soon she was galloping at full speed straight towards the big pot. She hit it headfirst with the big flat thick bone of her big wide head and sent the pot toppling over. When it toppled over, all of the water spilled out and ran like a river down the steep path that Tyrone and Albert were running up towards them.

As the river of water ran down the path lots of other little rivers seemed to join it and the path was turned into wet slippy sloppy mud. It became so slippery and sloppery that when Tyrone and Albert ran onto it, they slipped and slid about so much that they fell over. Then, the more they tried to stand up, the more they slipped and fell over, and the more they tried, the more they turned the path into even slippier and sloppier mud.

At the top of the steep path, Scary Bones and the children laughed and laughed as Tyrone and Albert slipped and fell about in the slippy sloppy mud.

'Right,' said Scary Bones. 'We must escape while we can. Dippy you go that way and Durdle will take us this way and back to where we first came into this lost world.'

After waving her long neck to say 'Good-bye' to everyone, Dippy trotted off into the trees. Scary Bones and the children and the Red String climbed onto Durdle's back and she began to trot back towards the cliff where they had first met.

As she trotted along between the trees Durdle Doorus was as happy as a happy hippopotamus again and she began to sing a happy song.

This is the happy song that Durdle began to sing :

> *'I'm busy being happy,*
> *Happy the whole day through,*
> *Happy because I've got friends such as you,*
> *I'm happy being happy,*
> *Happy and feeling fine,*
> *I'll never be unhappy again,*
> *Because of these friends of mine.*
> *Da, da, diddily da, diddily diddily diddily da.*

'That's a lovely song, Durdle,' said Scary Bones.

'Yes,' Durdle said, 'I'm always happy when I have children around me. I love to watch them having fun, playing games, climbing on my back, and just being happy. I wish that I could have happy children around me for ever and ever, and perhaps even longer than that.'

'Perhaps you will one day Durdle, perhaps one day your wish will come true,' said Scary Bones. 'But look out, be careful now, we don't want to fall into Ziggy and Zaggy's silly big dinosaur trap again do we?'

There, in the middle of the path right in front of them, was the great big hole that Ziggy and Zaggy had dug to catch dinosaurs. As they came nearer to it, they heard voices coming up from the bottom of the hole. As they passed by the hole they looked down into it and saw that there, down at the very bottom, were Ziggy and Zaggy!

'My word,' Scary Bones called down to them, 'Ziggy and Zaggy, how in the lost world have you been so silly as to fall into your own silly big hole again?'

'Well,' Zaggy called back. 'We knew a quick way to get here before you, and when we got here I told Ziggy that we must be careful not to fall into our big hole again.'

'But then,' Ziggy called out, 'when I tried to go past the hole, silly Zaggy zigged when he should have zagged and we bumped into each other and bumped each other into the hole.'

'Don't you call me silly!' said Zaggy. 'It's you that is silly. When I zigged you should have zagged.'

'Well, if I'm silly then you are even sillier,' said Ziggy. 'How did I know you were going to zig instead of zag? I was ziggy-zaggying quite nicely until you zigged when you should have zagged.'

'Ohhh, I was already zigging when you zigged,' said Zaggy, 'You should have zagged.'

'Oh no, you should have zagged, not zigged,' said Ziggy.

'Oh no,' said Zaggy, 'you should have zigged, not zagged. I was already zagging when you zagged.'

Scary Bones and the children knew that Ziggy and Zaggy would go on arguing like this for hours and so Scary Bones told Durdle to carry on walking.

'Goodbye Ziggy, goodbye Zaggy,' they called down into the hole as they went past. 'We expect that if you ever stop arguing Dippy will come along and get you out again. And remember to thank her and to be kind to her for ever and ever if she does.'

They hadn't gone far past the hole when they heard a great smashing and crashing and roaring and all other sorts of frightening noises coming from the path behind them. The children and Scary Bones turned around and looked down the path. It was Tyrone and Albert. They must have escaped from the slippery sloppery mud and were charging along the path towards them.

'Giddy yap Durdle,' Scary Bones shouted to Durdle Doorus. 'Giddy yap as fast as you can giddy yap. Tyrone and Albert are right behind us!'

Durdle Doorus began to giddy yap as fast as her big legs could giddy yap. *Cluumpetty, clumpetty, clumpetty, clumpetty.* Then, as she ran round a bend in the path, they saw that they were back at the cliff where they had first come through the giant door into the lost world. The cliff was right in front of them and Durdle Doorus was giddy yapping so fast that it seemed certain that she would crash into it.

'*Ssshhttttoooooopppppppp!*' They all shouted out together and Durdle Doorus slammed on whatever brakes she had. S*ccrrreeeecccccchhh! Bump*!

When she finally came to a stop, Durdle's big snout was just touching the cliff face.

'Well done, Durdle,' said Scary Bones, patting her on the head. 'Well done, no dinosaur in the whole wide lost world could have made such a quick stop.'

'Three cheers for Durdle Doorus,' Ben shouted.

'No time for that now, I'm afraid,' said Scary Bones. 'Look, here come Tyrone and Albert!'

Tyrone and Albert had come round the bend too and were still charging after them. With Tyrone and Albert so close behind them and the cliff right in front of them, there was ...... NO ESCAPE!

'Right,' said Durdle Doorus. 'Get behind me, I'm not afraid of these two big bullies. They will have to deal with me before they can eat you for their suppers!'

Durdle Doorus turned around to face the two monster dinosaurs. Tyrone and Albert stopped charging towards them. They didn't like the thought of having to fight someone as big as Durdle Doorus.

'Now come on, Durdle,' said Tyrone in a friendly voice. 'Don't be a silly-billy. We don't want to have a fight with you. We just want those three friends of yours for our supper and as soon as you give them to us we can all go back to our homes.'

'No, no, never,' said Durdle Doorus. 'These are my friends and I'll never give them up to you. I would rather die fighting you than betray my friends.'

'So be it,' said Albert. 'We have given you a chance and so now you will have only yourself to blame for whatever happens, because you know and we know, there is ...... NO ESCAPE! '

Tyrone and Albert began to claw at the ground with the big claws that were at the ends of their great big legs. They roared and roared so loudly that in their big open mouths their rows and rows of teeth glistened and shuddered in the sunlight. Then, just at the very moment they were about to charge, a small dinosaur dashed between Albert's legs heading straight towards the cliff. Flying and diving right behind it came a great big flying something-or-other that looked a bit like Terry Dactil except that it had feathers on its wings. It was clear that the flying something-or-other was chasing after the small dinosaur and was going to eat it for its supper if it could catch it.

Then, just as the flying whatever-it-was was about to catch it, the small dinosaur ran down what looked like a big rabbit hole at the bottom of the cliff.

'What in the lost world were those two?' Scary Bones asked Durdle Doorus.

'Well,' Durdle replied, 'the flying one with the feathers was Archie, Archie Opterix and the one he was chasing was Orytod Romus, we call him Ory for short. Archie would have eaten Ory if he had caught him.'

'It seems to me that everybody eats everybody else in this lost world,' Scary Bones said.

'Oh no, not everybody is like that. Dippy and I, for example, only eat plants,' Durdle replied. 'But you must be careful now. Archie will be very angry that his supper has escaped. He will come back to get you or the children for his supper! So, quickly now, you must all hide in Ory's big hole too. I'll stay here to keep the two monsters and Archie away from you.'

'But you'll never be able to ......'

Scary Bones started to answer but Durdle Doorus could see that Tyrone and Albert were getting ready to attack and that Archie was already diving down from the sky towards them.

'Shush, shush,' Durdle said. 'You must do as I say, and do it quickly.'

And so Scary Bones, the children and the Red String scrambled down into Ory's hole and into the darkness below. There seemed to be tunnels going off in all directions, here, there and everywhere, but one, which seemed as if it went right under the cliff face, had a sparkle of sunlight twinkling at the end of it. The Red String slithered off towards it and, in less time than it takes to go from here to there in a dark tunnel, it was dancing at the end of the tunnel in sparkling sunshine and waving to them to follow it.

The children and Scary Bones crawled along the dark black tunnel on their hands and knees towards where the sunlight was sparkling and where the Red String was waving to them. When they got to the end of the tunnel and stepped out into the sunshine, they found that they were back on the cliffs right where they had opened the giant door into the lost world that very morning.

Scary Bones and the children had escaped from the terrible monsters and the lost world, but they knew that they had only escaped because of the bravery of their good friend Durdle Doorus.

Chapter 7

'Poor Durdle Doorus,' said Ben. 'Is there anything we can do to save her from Tyrone and Albert?'

Sasha shook her head and said sadly, 'No, she is still behind these cliffs in the lost world and there's nothing we can do to save her now.'

'But there is,' Scary Bones shouted and he pointed a bony finger towards the cliffs. 'Look, the ammonite doorknob is still there!'

Sasha and Ben looked to where Scary Bones was pointing and saw that the ammonite doorknob was still sticking out from the cliffs exactly as they had first found it that very morning.

'Quickly, quickly,' said Sasha. 'If we can open the door again, Durdle Doorus will be able to escape from Tyrone and Albert.'

Ben and Scary Bones ran to the ammonite doorknob and then, holding it as tightly as they could, they began to turn it. Slowly but surely it began to turn and, as it turned, there was a mighty rumbling as loud as the loudest thunder in the stormiest of storms on the darkest of dark nights. The cliff *cc-ccrrraaaccked* and *cc-ccrrreeeeaaked* and *sh-sh-shuudderred*.

The whole cliff seemed to be making noises and moving and shaking all around where they stood. But this time they weren't frightened at all because they knew that it meant the giant stone door in the cliff was going to open again.

And so it did. The giant stone door opened wider and wider until it couldn't open any wider and it came to a stop with a mighty clump. *K-ker--rrlllluuummmppp*! As it clumped wide open all of the noises and rumblings came to a stop and the cliff became silent once more.

'Right,' said Scary Bones. 'You stay here to make sure that the door doesn't bang shut and lock me in the lost world again.' With that, Scary Bones ran through the doorway and back into the lost world. But would he be in time to save Durdle Doorus from the two dinosaur monsters, Tyrone and Albert?

Scary Bones got to Durdle Doorus just as Tyrone and Albert were getting ready to charge at her.

'Quickly, Durdle,' he called to her, 'follow me, we have found a way back into our world. You will be able to escape into it with us.'

Durdle Doorus turned to look at him and said very sadly, 'But I can't come with you. You see I am really millions and millions and millions of years old, and perhaps even older than that. If I should ever go into your world I would become a fossil and turn to solid stone.'

'Oh no!' said Scary Bones. 'What can we do? We can't leave you here alone.'

'You must,' said Durdle. You must go now. I'll be alright, you'll see. Please go and give my love to Sasha and Ben, and the Red String too.'

'I'll go then,' said Scary Bones sadly. 'But we will never forget you, I promise. Good bye my good friend Durdle, and good luck!' And Scary Bones turned and ran back through the stone door.

'Where is Durdle Doorus?' Ben and Sasha asked him when he came out. 'Why isn't she with you?'

'She can't come out here to be with us,' Scary Bones replied sadly. 'She is millions and millions and millions of years old, and so if she ever left the lost world to come into ours, she would turn into a fossil and become solid stone.'

Scary Bones and the children looked back through the giant doorway in the cliff. They could see that Tyrone and Albert were running and roaring straight towards Durdle Doorus. To protect herself, Durdle lowered her big wide head and the two monster dinosaurs crashed right into it. Because they were so very big and so very heavy, when Tyrone and Albert crashed into Durdle Doorus they bounced her right over and she came gambolling and bumping and bouncing out through the doorway and out into our world.

Tyrone and Albert began to run towards the doorway to chase after her and so, to stop them, the children slammed the giant door shut right in their big faces.

But when the children slammed the door, they slammed it so hard that the ammonite doorknob fell off and broke into thousands and thousands of tiny pieces on the rocks below.

Now that the ammonite doorknob had been smashed beyond repair, no-one would ever be able to use it to enter or leave the lost world again. At last they were safe from the monster dinosaurs of the lost world. They were just about to shout three cheers when they saw that Durdle Doorus was beginning to turn to stone, just like she had told Scary Bones she would.

Her great big body was rolling and bumping slowly down the cliffs towards the beach and the sea. As she rolled down the cliffs, more and more of her big body turned to stone. She was growing bigger and bigger too. In the lost world she hadn't grown for millions and millions and millions of years and so now she was growing to the size she would have grown to in our world. When she had grown to her full size, she started to become part of the cliffs around her and she slowly rolled to a stop on the beach.

Durdle Doorus tried to raise her head as if to say 'goodbye' but she couldn't. Almost every part of her had turned to stone. Her head was the last part of her to turn to stone and it was getting heavier and heavier. When she couldn't hold it up any longer, it sank lower and lower until her snout dipped into sea and her neck became like a bridge over it. When her snout dipped into the water the whole of Durdle Doorus had turned to stone and had become part of the cliffs around her.

Sasha and Ben eyes filled with tears and they began to cry. Scary Bones would have cried too but, as you know, skeletons can't cry because they don't have anywhere to store their tear drops. Even the Red String curled itself into a sad shape.

But as they looked down at Durdle Doorus and the golden sands of the beach and the bright blues of the sea and sky, the strangest of things began to happen. Children began to appear from here, there, everywhere and nowhere. Some began playing and laughing on the beach. Some began swimming in the sparkling blue water, and others began playing and climbing on the rocks and cliffs that had once been Durdle Doorus.

As he looked down, Scary Bones began to turn golden all over and he was smiling one of his biggest and toothiest smiles. Through their tears Sasha and Ben turned to him and asked,

'Why are you so happy Scary Bones, can't you see that our friend Durdle Doorus who saved us from Albert and Tyrone has turned into stone and rock? Why aren't you as sad as we are?'

'Well,' Scary Bones replied. 'You know that I am able to talk to anything that has a skeleton and, like all dinosaurs, Durdle Doorus had a skeleton inside her. Well, she once told me that she was at her happiest when she had children around her. She loved to watch them having fun, playing games, climbing on her back and being happy. Her greatest wish was that she could have happy children around her for ever and ever, and perhaps even longer than that.'

He stopped and pointed towards the children playing all around the cliffs and rocks that were once Durdle Doorus. 'And now, you see, her wish has come true and now she will be happy for ever and ever and perhaps even longer than that.'

Before they had chance to answer, Sasha and Ben heard their parents calling from somewhere on the beach.

'SASHA! BEN! Where are those children?'

'I'd better be going before they see me,' said Scary Bones and he and the Red String jumped into the grey box which was still lying on the rocks where it had been left. 'Goodbye,' Scary Bones said. 'That was another exciting adventure. I wonder where our next adventure will lead us.'

The children laughed. 'Yes, we wonder too. Good bye Scary Bones.' Then in an instant Scary Bones disappeared, as he always did, into a golden glow in the grey box and the Red String curled itself up and went to sleep in one of the corners. Ben picked up the box and he and Sasha began to walk towards where their parents were calling to them.

'Well there you are,' their parents said when they saw them. 'Have you had a good day? Did you find any fossils?'

'Yes,' said Sasha, 'look, I found this ammonite on the beach this morning,' and she held the ammonite out for her parents to see.

'My, that really is a super fossil but now, did you meet or see any dinosaurs?'

'A few,' Ben said, 'especially that one over there,' and he pointed towards Durdle Doorus.

His parents laughed. 'Oh, that's not a dinosaur,' they said, 'that's what people call Durdle Door. It's a very famous rock and people come from all over the world just to see it. Look, here is a photo of it to remind you of your holiday here.'

This is the photograph of Durdle Door
that Sasha and Ben's parents gave to them.

The children took the photograph but decided it was best not to tell their parents the real story of Durdle Door because they probably would never have believed it.

But those children who know the real story of Durdle Door tell of a magical thing that sometimes happens. They say that at the end of a beautiful summer's day, when all the people have left the cliffs and the sea and the beaches around Durdle Door, as the moon rises, if you look very closely you will see that Durdle Door seems to have a big smile and two bright eyes that twinkle high above the sea.

The children say that, when it happens, Durdle Door becomes Durdle Doorus again. Her smile and twinkling eyes tell us she is very very happy to be surrounded by so much happiness and to know that, because she is part of the cliffs, she will share her happiness with everyone for ever and ever, and perhaps just a little bit longer.

When Sasha and Ben arrived home, they wrote a letter to Scary Bones to tell him how famous their friend Durdle Doorus had become. They put the letter and the photograph of Durdle Door into an envelope and dropped it into Scary Bones' grey box.

As the envelope, with their letter in it, touched the bottom of the grey box, there was a little puff of white smoke and, when the smoke had drifted away into the air, the envelope had disappeared.

And do you know that from that day, when it disappeared behind that little puff of white smoke in the grey box, Sasha and Ben's letter to Scary Bones has never ever been seen again?

The End.

The author would like to record his sincere thanks to the pupils and teachers of Anderton Park School, Dunbury School, Milldown School, and Sandroyd School, and to all those friends, parents, teachers and other children who contributed to the publication of this story.

This is the fifth in 'The Amazing Adventures of Scary Bones the Skeleton' series. The other stories are :

The Lost Dog and Bone : This first adventure tells how Sasha and Ben meet Scary Bones and the Red String for the very first time. The town dogs have all disappeared and Scary Bones has lost a bone. In the adventure that follows they meet the terrible dog-nappers Snatchet and Grabbet, and Mrs. Grumble.

The Pirates of Brownsea Island : Scary Bones, Sasha and Ben are captured by pirates who are after old Captain Grow Bag's treasure which is buried on Brownsea Island. Helped by the island's Red Squirrels, our heroes save it for us all to enjoy for ever.

The Wacky Witches of Wareham : The children of Wareham have disappeared and the town is full of sleepy cats. Can Scary Bones rescue Sasha and Ben from the spell of two very strange and unusual lollipop ladies and keep the wizard of Corfe Castle from ruling the world?

The Nasty Romans of Maiden Castle : Our heroes are whisked back to Roman Britain by the Celtic Queen Do-you-see-her. They are captured by nasty Romans and made to fight two fierce gladiators and a lion in the arena. Can they escape and get back home again?

The Knights and Dragon of Durlston Head. In this adventure our heroes meet Princess Tilly Whim and her Knights Sir Moanalot and Sir Groanalot who are trying to rescue the Lord Loveydovey from Badtrix, a mad bad magician, and Volcano, his fire breathing dragon.

Every Scary Bones adventure has a mysterious sealed envelope that should not be opened until the end of the story.

MTBooks

Mulberry Tree Books, Mulberry House,
Winterborne Stickland, Dorset DT11 0NT

www.mulberrytreebooks.co.uk